Hello, you

Oh, please don't **look**
inside the pages
of this **book**.

DO NOT
EAT THIS
BOOK!

Turn around and
quickly **run** ...

The
SCHOOL
of
MONSTERS
has **begun!**

THIS BOOK
BELONGS TO

SCHOOL OF MONSTERS

By Sally Rippin

PIP LOVES TO COOK

Art by Chris Kennett

Kane Miller
A DIVISION OF EDC PUBLISHING

Pip loves to cook and loves to **bake**.

Today she makes
a big mud **cake**.

But Mrs. Black says,
"No more, **Pip**!

That's too much mud.
Someone might **slip**!

"Go wash your hands
inside with **Cook**,

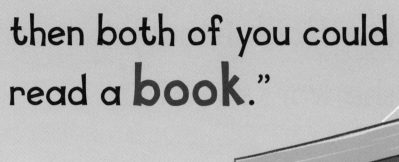

then both of you could read a **book**."

But Cook is busy,
she works **hard**.

CHOP
CHOP
CHOP

"Go fetch some things, Pip, from the **yard**.

9

"Take a cookbook,
have a **look**

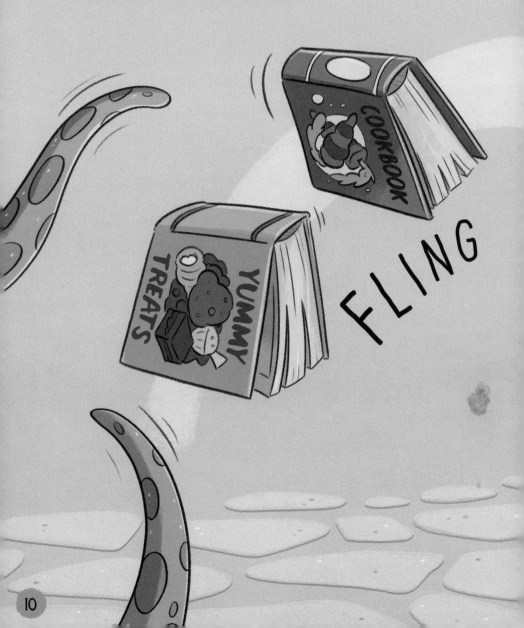

FLING

inside to see what we can **cook**."

Pip takes a cookbook from the **stack**

then grabs a bag,
heads out the **back**.

She fills the bag with lots of **things**:

berries, leaves, and bugs with **wings**.

Cook heats some water till it's **hot**.

Pip brings the bag
up to the pot.

Pip drops things in, it starts to **smell**.

Cook rushes back,
begins to **yell**.

"Oh no!" she says.
"You didn't **look**.

This book won't show
you how to **cook**!"

Pip starts to cry.
She feels so **bad**.

She didn't mean to
make Cook **mad.**

Cook tastes the soup.
What will she **think**?

"You know, it's *good,*
despite the **stink**!"

The lunch bell rings.
They all rush **in**.

Cook serves the soup
in bowls of **tin**.

The soup looks bad, but they don't **mind**!

Pip's monster friends are super **kind**.

"You know," says Cook,
"just like with **books,**

you can't judge food
by how it **looks!**"

stack

bad

think

hard

mad

look

bake

hot

books

Pip

kind

stink

book

yell

looks

pot

cake

slip

in

things

tin

wings

HOW TO USE THIS BOOK

for adults reading with children

Welcome to the School of Monsters!

Here are some tips for helping your child learn to read.

At first, your child will be happy just to listen to you read aloud. Reading to your child is a great way for them to associate books with enjoyment and love, as well as to become familiar with language. Talk to them about what is going on in the pictures and ask them questions about what they see. As you read aloud, follow the words with your finger from left to right.

Once your child has started to receive some basic reading instruction, you might like to point out the words in **bold**. Some of these will already be familiar from school. You can assist your child to decode the ones they don't know by sounding out the letters.

As your child's confidence increases, you might like to pause at each word in bold and let your child try to sound it out for themselves. They can then practice the words again using the list at the back of the book.

After some time, your child may feel ready to tackle the whole story themselves. Maybe they can make up their own monster stories, too!

Sally Rippin is one of Australia's best-selling and most-beloved children's authors. She has written over 50 books for children and young adults, and her mantel holds numerous awards for her writing. Best known for her *Billie B. Brown*, *Hey Jack!* and *Polly and Buster* series, Sally loves to write stories with heart, as well as characters that resonate with children, parents, and teachers alike.

HOW TO DRAW PIP

① Using a pencil, start with 2 circles for eyes, a smiley mouth, and oval-shaped head.

② Add some loops for the hair and collar, some half circles for ears, and curvy lines for the hair bunches.

③ Draw 2 lines for the body and 4 loops for the bottom of the dress.

④ Add some lines for arms and legs, leaving the ends open.

⑤ Draw in the hands and feet.

⑥ Time for the final details! Draw in some eyelashes, lines for her bracelets, belt, and leggings. Don't forget her two front teeth!

Chris Kennett has been drawing ever since he could hold a pencil (or so his mom says). But professionally, Chris has been creating quirky characters for just over 20 years. He's best known for drawing weird and wonderful creatures from the *Star Wars* universe, but he also loves drawing cute and cuddly monsters – and he hopes you do too!

WELCOME TO THE  SCHOOL of MONSTERS

Have you read **ALL** the School of Monsters stories?

START HERE

You shouldn't bring a pet to **school**. But Mary's pet is super **cool**!

Sam makes a mess when he eats **jam**. Can he fix it? Yes, he **can**!

Today it's Sports Day in the **sun**. But do you think that Pete can **run**?

When Bug starts school he cannot **read**. But teacher has the help he **needs**!

This is Jem. She likes to **play**, and thinks up fun new ways each **day**!

"Why won't Bruno dance?" says **Pat**. "There must be a fix for **that**!"

Pip loves to cook and loves to **bake**. But will the monsters like her **cake**?

NEXT LEVEL

Jamie Lee sure likes to **eat!** Today she has a special **treat** ...

When Bat-Boy Tim comes out to **play**, why do others run **away**?

WELL DONE

No one likes to be left **out**. This makes Luna scream and **shout!**

When Will gets nervous, he lets out a **stink**. But what will all his classmates **think**?

Some monsters are short, and others are **tall**, but Frank is quite clearly the tallest of **all!**

All that Jess touches gets gooey and **sticky**. How can she solve a problem so **tricky**?

MORE MONSTERS COMING SOON!

Now that you've learned to read along with Sally Rippin's School of Monsters, meet her other friends!

Hey Jack!

Billie B. Brown

Down-to-earth, real-life stories for real-life kids!

Billie B. Brown is brave, brilliant and bold,
and she always has a creative way to save the day!

Jack has a big heart and an even bigger imagination.
He's Billie's best friend, and he'd love to be your friend, too!

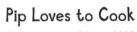

Pip Loves to Cook

First American Edition 2023
Kane Miller, A Division of EDC Publishing

All rights reserved.
For information contact:
Kane Miller, A Division of EDC Publishing
5402 S 122nd E Ave, Tulsa, OK 74146
www.kanemiller.com

Library of Congress Control Number: 2022952273

ISBN: 978-1-68464-749-1

Printed in China
10 9 8 7 6 5 4 3 2 1